Star-Crossed Love

GW00391067

Chapter One

Blair Young put her book facedown on the coffee table, then stood up and stretched. She had been rereading *Romeo and Juliet* for the upcoming school play and had been so absorbed in the story that it took her a moment to remember where she was.

She walked into the dining room and stared at herself in the mirror over the buffet, trying to envision herself as Juliet. Blair studied her reflection. She was taller than most of the girls her age, and very slender. Her blond hair was ruler straight, although it was thick and shiny and fell well below her shoulders. "You have good hair—it's healthy," her mother would say when Blair complained that it was boring. But Juliet had dark hair, and just then, Blair wished she did, too.

She moved closer to the mirror and opened her eyes wide. They were dark brown, with heavy black lashes, and everyone said they were her best feature. Blair grimaced, noticing her fair skin. Then she shrugged—at least she could cover it with makeup. *After all,* Romeo and Juliet *is a play, not a look-alike contest,* she thought.

"Doing your ape imitation, Bean?" Bean was the nickname Blair's eleven-year-old brother, Peter, had given her. It was short for Bean Pole.

Blair whirled around. Her brother was grinning at her from the doorway.

"Do you have to sneak up on people, Peter?" she said coldly.

"I didn't sneak up on you. I'm ten feet away from you." He came a few steps closer. "Why were you making all those faces in the mirror?"

"Mind your own business," Blair snapped. Sometimes she hated having a younger brother. Why couldn't she have had an older brother, someone she could talk to and who would understand her? She walked down the hallway to the guest room where her grandmother was sitting by the window, knitting.

"Hi, Gram," Blair leaned down to kiss the older woman's soft cheek, which was lightly etched with age. She smiled, thinking how glad she was that Gram had been able to come for such a long visit this time.

"Hello, dear. I didn't realize you were home."

"I was in the living room reading *Romeo and Juliet.* We're putting it on at school, and the auditions are on Thursday. I can hardly wait!" Blair sat down on the edge of the bed and curled her legs up under her. "I just know I'm going to get to play Juliet."

Her grandmother smiled. "You're awfully confident, just as your mother was twenty years ago."

"And she got it, didn't she?" Blair replied. "I saw the picture of her in her costume."

"Yes, she did. She was such a lovely Juliet. Of course, the school was so small that she was also the only girl who tried out for the part. You'll probably have more competition."

Blair frowned. "But, Gram, Pine River High is lots smaller than my old school. And I don't know anyone in my drama class who's even going out for the part. Besides, we studied the play in my English class last year, and I know all of Juliet's lines."

Blair's grandmother cocked her head. "Never be too confident, dear. You're apt to be disappointed."

Blair laughed and shook her head. "Nowadays you're supposed to think positively and your dreams will come true."

"Is that what you young people learn these days?"

Blair reached over to pat her grandmother's hand. "Don't worry, Gram, we'll turn out all right." She stood up and stretched. "Well, I guess I'd better go put the roast on for dinner. Mom said she'll be home about six. Who knows when Dad will finish up."

Blair's father was the basketball and track coach at Pine River High. He had taken the job at the beginning of the school year, moving his family to California from a much larger town in northwestern Washington. Blair had been miserable at first. She'd hated having to move to a new school for her sophomore year. But now, six months later, she had grown to love her new home.

Blair had made a few friends during the first semester of school, and the move to Pine River had been softened by the arrival of a new drama teacher at the high school. Mr. Stanley had only been out of college a few years, and he'd worked with several small theater groups before he decided to teach. He was young and energetic, and his classes were very popular. Blair often stopped by Mr. Stanley's office after school to talk to him about the theater, because he encouraged her interest in acting.

After putting the roast in the oven for her mother, who worked long hours as a nurse at Pine River Hospital, Blair grabbed up her books

4

and headed up to her room to study. She sat down at her desk, opened up her geometry book, and started working on her assignment. But soon her mind wandered. She closed her geometry book and picked up her worn copy of *Romeo and Juliet*. She thumbed through Act I until she came across the line where Juliet tells her nurse: "*Go ask his name.*"

Blair stared dreamily out the window. She was almost certain Shane Lawson would be cast as Romeo. He was the best-looking boy in the junior class, and he was also in her drama class. He would be a perfect Romeo—tall, with dark, wavy hair and wonderful hazel eyes. The thought of Shane Lawson made Blair slightly breathless. He was *so* good-looking.

Shane was also one of Blair's father's star basketball players. She had gone to all the games just to see him play. Whenever they had a game, Blair and her best friend, Frances Barker, would sit in the front row of the bleachers, rooting loudly. And after the game, she would hang around her father before the team left for the locker room, hoping to see Shane. Occasionally, he would smile and say hi to her, but Blair had never really talked to him.

On the way home from the game the week before, Peter had nudged Blair in the side with his elbow. Then he said very loudly, "Blair's got a crush on Shane Lawson. I saw her staring at him."

Blair's cheeks had burned with embarrassment, and she was glad the car was dark. "I was watching the game, Peter," she'd answered in an icy voice. "If you knew anything about basketball, you'd know that Shane Lawson is Dad's best forward."

"That's true," Mr. Young commented, ignoring Peter's remark, "but the one who is going to win the title for us this year is Charlie McGuire. He's one of the best centers I've ever coached."

Charlie McGuire was in Blair's drama class, too. He was taller than Shane, and he seemed to be all legs and arms. But Blair could see that he had enormous grace on the court. And even though Charlie was almost as cute as Shane— with curly red hair and dazzling green eyes—it was his sense of humor that people remembered. He was always friendly, too. Blair wished Shane Lawson were as friendly to her as Charlie was. She smiled to herself. Maybe playing Romeo and Juliet together would help bring them closer.

That night at dinner, Blair reminded her parents that the auditions for *Romeo and Juliet* would be on Thursday and that she was hoping to get the part of Juliet.

"I'm not sure who's trying out for Romeo," she went on innocently. "There are quite a few boys in our class, and Mr. Stanley also announced the tryouts in the English classes. There'll probably be a lot of kids there."

"I want Shane Lawson to be my Romeo," Peter said in a high-pitched voice.

Blair glared at him.

"Actually, several of the guys on the team are talking about trying out," said Mr. Young. "Shane is one of them. I also heard Charlie saying that he was going to audition for Romeo."

"Charlie McGuire?" said Blair incredulously. "A red-haired Romeo?"

"A red-haired Romeo?" Peter mimicked.

"Peter, please," Mrs. Young remonstrated. She looked at Blair fondly. "I think that's wonderful, Blair. *Romeo and Juliet* is such a good introduction to Shakespeare. And I'm sure Mr. Stanley will do a fine job of directing." She bit her lip and paused. "But Blair, dear, try not to be disappointed if you don't get cast as Juliet. It's not being the star, it's just being a part of the production that counts."

"Oh, I know, Mom," Blair said in an impatient tone. "'But no one else knows the part as well as I do. Mr. Stanley practically told me I'd get the part." She paused, then added, "Well, he told me I had a good chance to get it."

Blair jumped up and started stacking the empty plates. She didn't want any more cautious advice—or any stupid comments from her brother. "I'll clear the table now, Mom. I've got to get back to my geometry." She sucked in her breath and squeezed between Peter's chair and the buffet.

The next morning before she left for school, Blair kissed her grandmother good-bye. Mrs. Young was taking her mother to the airport to put her on a flight home to eastern Washington.

"I'll write to you about the auditions, Gram," Blair said. "Won't you be happy to have another Juliet in the family?"

"Of course." Her grandmother nodded. "But remember what I said, Blair. Don't be disappointed if things don't work out the way you expect them to."

Blair glanced at her mother, whose expression told her not to argue. She hugged her grandmother and smiled.

"Everything will work out fine, Gram." Blair slipped out the kitchen door before her grandmother could add any more words of wisdom.

Adults are so cautious, she thought as she headed down the street to meet Frances. Blair glanced up at the pine-covered hills that rose in the distance. They were capped with snow, even though it was warm for February.

Frances met her a couple of blocks from school, and the two girls walked along talking excitedly about the auditions.

"I'm sure you'll be cast as Juliet," Frances said. "You're easily the best actress in the class."

"Thanks, Fran. At least someone's being optimistic. Everyone at home keeps telling me not to be disappointed if I don't get it."

"Well, who else could play Juliet?" Frances reasoned. "*I'm* really not much of an actress, and neither are a lot of the girls in our class."

Blair looked at her friend. *Poor Frances,* she thought, *she really doesn't know what a good actress she is.*

"Pam and Laura want to try out for the parts of the mothers," Frances continued, "and there aren't many other female parts."

"Well, there's the nurse," Blair suggested. "That's a pretty big part."

"Who wants to be the nurse?" Frances frowned. "She's so old."

"Fran, it's a great part. The nurse is one of the most interesting characters in the whole play," argued Blair.

"Really? Maybe I will audition for the nurse," Frances said after thinking for a moment.

"Good!" The warning bell rang, and the two girls hurried toward their homerooms.

That afternoon in drama class, Mr. Stanley

asked the students to get out their copies of *Romeo and Juliet.* He leaned casually against his desk and glanced around the room.

"Today, I want to discuss *Romeo and Juliet.* I hope you have all read it," Mr. Stanley went on, looking from student to student, "because in order to dramatize Shakespeare successfully, we need to understand the language thoroughly. While it's beautiful and lyrical, Shakespeare is also archaic and difficult to understand at first." He paused and smiled at the class. "So, who has any questions about the play?"

Everyone was quiet for a minute. Then Charlie McGuire raised his hand, and Mr. Stanley called on him.

"What made you choose this particular play? I know it's romantic and all that, but it's been done a million times."

"That's a good question, Charlie," Mr. Stanley answered. "To be quite honest, I chose *Romeo and Juliet* for the audience. I checked with some of the other teachers, and I discovered that no Shakespeare has ever been done here before. I thought this play might be a good introduction to Shakespeare for the community."

"Because it's the most well known?" Charlie asked.

"Exactly," said Mr. Stanley.

"That makes sense"—Charlie's smile broadened—"especially to all us Romeos."

Everyone laughed. Mr. Stanley chuckled, too. Then he looked at Eric Johnson.

"What strikes you first when you read *Romeo and Juliet*, Eric? What can you relate to?"

Blair looked at Frances out of the corner of her eye. She knew that Frances had a crush on Eric. Now, Frances was smiling shyly to herself, waiting anxiously for Eric to reply.

"Well, I kept thinking how Romeo and Juliet acted a lot like kids do today." He paused and grinned; there were a few giggles. "They're so impatient and moody."

"Give us an example, Eric." urged Mr. Stanley.

But Eric just shrugged and shook his head. Suddenly Charlie raised his hand, then started talking eagerly before Mr. Stanley called on him.

"Well, take Romeo. In the beginning of the play, he's moping around over Rosaline. Then his friends talk him into going to the party at the Capulets, and he falls flat on his face for Juliet. Rosaline's out of his head forever."

Everyone laughed at Charlie's comment.

"Well said, Charlie. I certainly hope you try out for a part. You seem to have a real feel for the play."

"Don't you think I'm a natural as Romeo— typecast, as they say?" Charlie joked. Charlie was constantly kidding around in class, and occasionally he got in trouble for it. But that day Blair could see that his jokes were making everyone relax.

"You'd make a great Mercutio," Frances said to him. "You've got the sense of humor for it."

Blair raised her hand, and Mr. Stanley nodded to her.

"I read once that some critics think Shakespeare had to kill Mercutio before he stole the show from Romeo." She looked at Charlie, hoping he saw that as a compliment. Instead, Charlie pointed dramatically at both Blair and Frances, " *'A plague on both your houses.'* "

Blair giggled, and laughter ran through the classroom. Then a girl Blair hardly knew spoke up.

"Juliet is childish in some ways, too. I mean, look at the way she relies on her nurse. And she's so afraid of her parents."

"But she sure is certain about wanting to marry Romeo," someone else argued.

"Maybe she thought of Romeo as just a way out of marrying old Paris."

"She wouldn't have killed herself over him if he were just a way to get away from Paris."

Pretty soon, everyone was talking at once. After a while, Mr. Stanley held up his hand to quiet them down.

"Good. I can see most of you have read the play carefully. And getting back to our original discussion, it's true that *Romeo and Juliet* is a story of impatient young love."

"If they hadn't been in such a hurry to get married, maybe they might have lived," suggested Shane.

"No, it was fated," said Blair. Then she wished she hadn't contradicted him.

"Good, Blair," Mr. Stanley said. "Where do we see that first?"

"In the prologue. *'A pair of star-crossed lovers take their life.'* "

"Good, and where else do we see this inevitability?"

"Doesn't Romeo say something about having a premonition before he goes to the party?" Charlie asked.

Blair looked at him. "You mean, *'I fear, too early; for my mind misgives / Some consequence yet hanging in the stars.'* "

"That's it." Charlie looked at her appreciatively. "You sure know the lines, Blair."

"Yeah," Shane agreed, smiling at Blair. "You'd be a good Juliet."

Blair blushed and mumbled, "We studied it last year in my English class." But in spite of her modesty, Blair was thrilled at Shane's compliment.

"Aren't there any plays of Shakespeare's that are easier to understand?" a boy in the back row asked, shaking his head.

Mr. Stanley smiled. "There's always a problem with the language until you've read several of Shakespeare's plays. But once we begin to dramatize it, I think you'll find it easier to understand."

Mr. Stanley kept them talking about the play until the bell rang. Blair was waiting for Frances to pack her books in her backpack when Shane walked up to her. He was smiling, and he looked so handsome that it made Blair's knees feel wobbly.

"Gosh, Blair, you're incredible. I really hope you get to play Juliet. You'd be so good."

Blair was just about to thank Shane when Charlie McGuire called out from behind him. "Boy, am I impressed, Blair. You know the play so well, Mr. Stanley should get you to help him direct."

Blair turned toward Charlie. "I don't know the play *that* well. Besides, I really love acting."

But Mr. Stanley, who had overheard the conversation, agreed with Charlie. "I do need a student assistant. Think about it, Blair. Directing is good experience if you like the theater."

Blair shook her head and shot a withering glance at Charlie, who just smiled back innocently. Then the two girls hurried to their next class, talking rapidly about the class discussion.

"I could just kill Charlie for saying I should help direct," Blair said.

"But he's right, you know," Frances said gently. "You really understand the play, and I'm sure you'd be a good assistant director." But when she looked at Blair's angry expression, she added hastily, "But you'd make a great Juliet, too."

That evening, Blair told her parents about the discussion in Mr. Stanley's class. "Everyone is so enthusiastic about the play. It should be really fun."

"Who else is trying out for Juliet?" her mother asked.

"No one. At least, no one in our drama class has said anything," Blair smiled.

"Then I guess you don't have to worry about the auditions," her father joked.

"Well," Blair said, "I hope Mr. Stanley will choose me because I'm good, not because there's no one else."

"And conceited," Peter mumbled. Blair glared at him.

"Peter . . ." Mr. Young said in a stern voice. Then he turned back to Blair. "I heard Charlie and Shane talking today with Eric Johnson about your class discussion. They seemed excited, too."

"I know Shane is. He even said I'd make a good Juliet," Blair announced proudly. Then she frowned. "But sometimes Charlie McGuire is such a pain. He said I should be the assistant director—right in front of Mr. Stanley!"

"I'm sure he meant it as a compliment, dear," Mrs. Young said.

"I'll bet! He probably knows how much I want to act, and—"

"Just relax, Blair," Mr. Young said. "*Romeo and Juliet* won't begin or end your career."

Just then the phone rang, and Peter ran to get it. "Hey, Bean, it's for you. It's a *boy*!" he shouted.

"Oh, Peter!" muttered Blair as she went to pick up the hall extension phone.

"Hello," she said in a careful voice. She half expected it to be Shane asking if she wanted to practice for the auditions with him. But instead it was Charlie.

"Hi, Blair. It's Charlie."

"Yes, Charlie," said Blair in a cool voice.

"Listen, I know you're going out for Juliet—and—well, I'm going to audition for Romeo." There was a pause while he took a breath. "So, I was thinking maybe we could practice together tomorrow night."

Blair was silent. She didn't want to practice with Charlie, and she didn't want him to get the part of Romeo.

"Well . . ." she said slowly, stalling so she could make up a good excuse.

"See, Blair, Shane's trying out for Romeo, too. And he's practicing with Margie Mason because she's trying out for Juliet. So," Charlie went on, "we should practice together if we want to get the parts."

Blair's heart stopped. Not Margie Mason. Not perfect, beautiful, snobby Margie Mason. Blair's shoulders slumped.

"Blair?" Charlie persisted. "What do you say?"

Blair took a deep breath and reminded herself that Margie Mason couldn't act. She hadn't expressed any interest in the two previous short performances they had done at school. She wasn't even in their drama class.

"Blair, are you there?" Charlie's voice had turned hesitant.

"All right, Charlie," Blair said at last. "All right. Let's practice tomorrow night." Her voice was flat and determined. Charlie seemed to pick up on it.

"Great! Is your house OK?"

"Yeah," Blair replied listlessly.

"I'll be there about seven. OK?"

"Yeah," Blair repeated.

" 'Bye, Blair," said Charlie.

" 'Bye, Charlie." She hung up the phone and walked back into the dining room. Her mother was clearing the table.

"Hey, Bean," Peter called from the living room, "a little competition, huh?"

Blair wheeled around. "You little creep! You were listening to me on the other phone." Her anger about Margie and Shane suddenly boiled over at Peter. "Mother!" she wailed.

"Peter," Mrs. Young said, "I've told you a million times how rude it is to listen in on the extension. Go upstairs!"

"Yes, ma'am," said Peter, walking toward the stairs. He looked at Blair with a grin. She could tell he wasn't sorry at all.

Blair started to gather up the dishes slowly.

Mrs. Young sensed her dejection. "Someone else is going out for Juliet?" she asked quietly.

Blair nodded.

"Don't worry, dear. You've had a lot of drama experience. Mr. Stanley knows that."

Blair didn't answer, and for the rest of the evening she didn't bring up the play.

Chapter Two

"Fran," Blair asked as they walked to school the next morning, "did you know that Margie Mason is trying out for Juliet?"

Frances looked at her in surprise. "No," she answered. "Who told you that?"

"Charlie. He called to ask if I'd rehearse with him tonight. He said Margie and Shane are trying out for *Romeo and Juliet*, and they're practicing together."

"Don't worry," Fran said in a soft voice. "She probably won't know the play at all. I'm sure you'll be Mr. Stanley's first choice."

Blair looked at her, trying to muster up a smile of thanks. "You've lived here all your life, Fran. Has Margie ever been in any school productions?"

"Umm," Frances said slowly. "No, not in high school."

"I mean ever?"

"Well, yeah. In grammar school she was Snow White. But you know how kids' plays are. And she was something in the eighth-grade play, but I can't remember."

"Was she good?"

"I can't remember, Blair."

Blair looked at her doubtfully.

"Honest, I can't. She must not have been too great or I would remember."

"Forget it. I'm just worried because I'm sure Shane will get Romeo, and if they practice together—"

"You think it will be you and Charlie against Shane and Margie?"

Blair nodded.

"Why don't you try to talk Charlie into trying out for Mercutio instead? Would that help?"

"No. What am I supposed to say? I tried to encourage him in class yesterday when I said that about Shakespeare killing Mercutio off."

"Well, tell him that Mercutio's *much* more interesting than Romeo. Romeo's really kind of a wimp."

"Frances!" Blair laughed because her friend never used words like *wimp*. Laughing made

20

Blair feel better. She gave Frances a smile of thanks as they entered the school grounds.

Margie Mason was in Blair's English class, but they had barely spoken two words to each other since school started. Margie had grown up in Pine River, and she was one of the most popular girls in school. She had been a homecoming princess that year and was a junior cheerleader. But Blair had never cared about those things, so Margie had never bothered her much—until she saw Margie walking with Shane Lawson, that is. And now that Margie was rehearsing with him, Blair looked on her as the enemy. As she entered the English classroom, Margie gave Blair a nasty look, and Blair had the sudden feeling that Margie knew Blair had a crush on Shane.

After class, Margie walked over to Blair's desk.

"I hear you're going out for Juliet?"

Blair looked at Margie's pretty face and long dark hair. She groaned inwardly. "Yes."

"And Charlie McGuire is your Romeo?"

Blair didn't answer as Margie laughed and walked off to join some girls who were waiting for her in the hall. Blair could hear them giggling.

Charlie McGuire . . . my Romeo? The blood rushed to Blair's face. *Is that what he's telling people?*

That afternoon, Blair walked angrily into drama class. She was going to have it out with Charlie. When he arrived a few seconds before the bell rang, he grinned at her.

"Hi, Juliet!"

Blair stormed over to him and said in a low voice, "What do you mean by telling everyone that you and I are going to be Romeo and Juliet?"

Charlie's eyes widened. "Oh, that was yesterday. And all I said was that we were going to rehearse together." He looked at Blair's flushed face. "What's the matter? You look like you're going to have a stroke."

Before Blair could answer, Shane Lawson walked up to Charlie and slapped him on the back. "Decided you're not such a Romeo after all, huh?"

Charlie jumped backward and grabbed a ruler from Mr. Stanley's desk. He bent his knees, faking a fencing pose and thrusting the ruler at Shane, who jumped out of the way, laughing.

" 'I will bite thee by the ear for that jest,' " said Charlie in a deep, theatrical voice. Everyone in the class broke up in laughter.

Blair was so relieved to hear that Charlie was not going out for Romeo that she, too, laughed. The class was still giggling when Mr. Stanley came in.

"I'm glad to see this play is generating so much enthusiasm," he said, sitting on the edge of his desk. "I have the sign-up sheets here for the tryouts, and I'll read off the names to you."

Lots of kids from outside their drama class were trying out, but Blair and Margie were still the only candidates for Juliet. Shane saw three competitors for Romeo, and Frances and several other girls were trying out for either Lady Capulet or Lady Montague.

"Charlie, I'm glad you decided to sign up for Mercutio."

" *'Why, is not this better now than groaning for love?'* " Charlie joked.

The class laughed again, and Mr. Stanley grinned. "You even know your lines."

"I read the play over last night and decided Mercutio was a much better role for my fencing skills."

Blair giggled. She was feeling much better. Charlie would make a great Mercutio, and now Shane was a shoo-in as Romeo.

"Well, Charlie," said Mr. Stanley, "your talent has scared everyone off. No one else has signed up."

They spent the class hour talking about the sets and the rehearsal schedule. Opening night was set for April fifteenth. Blair glanced over at Shane. He happened to be looking around the room at that moment, and their eyes met. He smiled, and Blair nearly melted. She was going to act her heart out at the audition. She had to get the part.

Charlie showed up that night just after Blair had loaded the dinner dishes into the dishwasher. He had met Blair's mother and brother at a basketball game and greeted them affably. Blair could see that Peter admired Charlie, because he was unusually quiet as he listened while Mr. Young talked to Charlie about the day's practice. The first play-off game was to take place Saturday, and if Pine River won, they would go to the finals the following week.

"If any of you get parts in the play, we'll have to rearrange our practice schedule before the finals," Mr. Young said.

"Thanks for understanding, Mr. Young," Charlie replied. "But that's only if we win the game Saturday *and* get cast."

"You bet," said Mr. Young with a nod.

Blair and Charlie went down to the basement, which had been turned into a family room. Peter followed them downstairs.

"Forget it, Peter. This is our practice, and I don't want your stupid comments."

"Aw, Bean, please! I won't say a thing, honest!"

"No!"

"Just let me see Charlie do his part."

Blair was about to say no again, but Charlie interrupted. "It's OK, Blair. I don't care if he watches." He winked at her. "After all, I'm a shoo-in. No one else is going out for the part."

"All right," she said grudgingly to Peter. "But only for Charlie's part. Then you have to go upstairs."

Peter nodded and settled into the old beanbag chair on the floor.

"OK, Charlie, where do you want to start?" Blair said.

Charlie frowned. "What do you think I should do? The Queen Mab part?"

"That's just what I was thinking. It's a good speech. Here, I'll be Romeo."

Charlie nodded, then he looked at Peter. "You probably won't understand the fancy language, Peter, but in this part Mercutio"—he pointed to himself—"that's me, is trying to talk Romeo into going to a party. But Romeo doesn't want to go. He talks about the dreams and premonitions he's had that something bad will happen. So"—Charlie took a deep breath—"Mercutio makes up this speech about a fairy named Queen Mab who makes people dream. He tries to make Romeo understand that dreams aren't warnings or messages, but just random thoughts."

Blair stared at Charlie. "Gosh, you really are

25

into this play. I know it because we studied it last year, but I needed a lot of help from the teacher." Blair smiled at Charlie with new respect.

Charlie shrugged and looked a little embarrassed. "Well, I really didn't understand it when Mr. Stanley first assigned it. It was just sort of double talk. But then I read the notes in the book and got another book out of the library that explained a lot of Shakespeare's plays. After a while, it started to make sense."

Blair went over to Charlie. "OK, I'll give Romeo's cue line. We should probably walk around the room as you speak to get the illusion of Mercutio, Benvolio, and Romeo going somewhere while they are talking." Blair glanced in her book, then stepped back and looked at Charlie. " *'In bed asleep, while they do dream things true.'* "

Charlie started the speech confidently, gesturing with ease. He was very convincing. And he didn't make one mistake, even when he jumped up on the sofa and walked along it as if he were balancing on a stone wall. Blair was so involved in his speech that she lost her cue. Charlie paused and said with a grin: "Merry lass, watch your lines."

Blair blushed and glanced down at her book.

" 'Peace, peace, Mercutio, peace! Thou talk'st of nothing.' "

Charlie then continued, jumping down off the couch and circling Blair. When he had finished, Blair and Peter both clapped.

"You were great, Charlie," Blair said. "You'd get the part even if ten guys were up for it."

"I think I'll go to this play," Peter said in an awed voice.

Charlie laughed, but Blair just pointed toward the stairs. "Out, Peter!" she commanded.

"Aw . . ." Peter started to protest, but Blair nodded her head firmly. Peter scowled and went upstairs, slamming the door behind him.

"You should have let him stay, Blair," said Charlie. "He might learn something."

Blair sighed. "He's not your brother. And he'd just make fun of me." She looked at her book. "What part should I do?"

"Probably the balcony scene," Charlie suggested. "That's what Margie's doing."

Blair frowned. "I don't have to do it just because she is."

"I know, but it's the most well known, so it's the easiest to judge." Charlie looked at Blair with a mischievous smile. "You could even ask Mr. Stanley to let Shane play opposite you when you try out."

"Shane?" Blair asked, confused. "Why Shane?"

"Come on, Blair." Charlie laughed. "I know you've got a thing for him."

Blair blushed and looked away, but Charlie continued good-naturedly. "That's OK. All the girls like Shane. I've gone all through school with him, and it's been going on for years."

Blair still said nothing. Charlie was right, of course, but she didn't realize her feelings were so obvious.

Charlie sensed her uneasiness and gave her a pat on the shoulder. The gesture was awkward, but it was meant to be kind. And it did make Blair feel a little better.

"It's OK, Blair," Charlie repeated. "Shane's a good guy. It's not like he's the Big Bad Wolf or something."

Blair laughed. "Oh, Charlie!"

She took a deep breath and ran through the balcony scene. The first couple of times, she made mistakes and ended up stamping her foot in frustration.

"Come on, Blair," Charlie coaxed. "Just relax."

"Why am I so nervous?"

"Maybe it's not nervousness. Maybe you aren't convinced of what you're saying." Charlie looked around the room. "I'll tell you what. Get up on that chair as if it were the balcony, and I'll kneel so you can just see the top of my head. Pretend I'm Shane."

Blair gave him a doubtful look, but she climbed

up on the chair anyway. She looked down at Charlie's red hair and began to giggle.

"Stop it, you jerk!" Charlie called.

Blair suppressed her laughter and took a deep breath. Then she began. It worked. She went through the entire speech without making a mistake. Her pauses and gestures were perfect; and when she was finished, Charlie stood up and gave her his hand to help her off the chair.

"Great! You were terrific!"

"Well, I'd better get it on the first try tomorrow or I won't get the part."

"You'll get it," he reassured her.

Charlie was nice, Blair decided. She was glad she'd agreed to practice with him. Now she understood why he was so popular at school.

"Charlie's not only a good athlete and a good sport, but he keeps the team's morale up with his disposition," Blair's father had said one time.

Now Charlie stretched his long legs out on the sofa and looked at Blair. "Are you really nervous?"

"I wish I looked more like Juliet, that's all," she said. "You know, with dark hair and all . . ."

"You don't need dark hair," said Charlie. "Juliet wears a cap. No one will see the color of your hair."

"Except Romeo," said Blair in a wistful voice.

"Oh, yeah. That's right. Shane hates blondes.

He told me he thinks all blondes are pale and ugly."

Blair stared at Charlie, her eyes wide with shock.

"Calm down, Blair, I was just kidding. Shane wouldn't say that. I just made it up." Charlie smiled. "And, anyway, you've got beautiful eyes."

Blair softened. "I'm sorry, Charlie. I guess I'm a little edgy tonight."

"Well, I'll leave so you can get to sleep early." He got up and stretched. "You're going to do fine, Blair. Think positively!"

Blair smiled, remembering how confident she had been when she had told her grandmother she was auditioning. She was glad Charlie was there to bolster her confidence. He was a good friend.

"Thanks, Charlie. At least we know *you're* going to get the part."

"And so are you!" Charlie persisted.

He said good night to Blair's parents, and they wished him good luck at the auditions. At the door Charlie turned and smiled again at Blair. "Don't worry about a thing," he said. Then he disappeared down the steps.

The next morning, Blair felt much better. She remembered Charlie's advice to think positively, and she was very cheerful at breakfast—so cheerful that her family looked at her strangely.

"What's the matter with you, Bean?" Peter asked.

Blair gave him an exasperated look and went into the bathroom to check herself one last time in the mirror. It was another frosty morning, so Blair had decided to wear a soft pink turtleneck sweater her mother had given her for Christmas. And instead of her usual blue jeans, she put on a pair of nubby wool pants that she'd only worn a couple of times. Blair wanted to look casual but serious. On the way to school, Frances told her that she looked very nice, and Blair took it as a good omen.

"How was your practice with Charlie?" Frances asked.

"It was fun. Charlie's going to be a great Mercutio, and he really helped me get into my part." Blair giggled, remembering Charlie kneeling at the foot of her chair. "You know how funny Charlie can be."

Frances nodded. "He's been that way since kindergarten. Even then he was the funniest kid in class. When I was in grammar school I even thought that all redheads were funny because Charlie had red hair."

"What about you, Fran?" Blair asked. "Do

you know your lines for Lady Capulet and Lady Montague?"

"I've changed my mind, Blair. I'm going to audition for the nurse."

"But, Fran," Blair protested, "you said you didn't like that part. Why don't you try out for Lady Capulet. It's a good role, too. I'll bet you'd be great."

Frances shook her head. "Pam and Laura want the mothers' parts, and I don't really care what part I get. It's being involved that counts."

Blair admired Frances's selflessness. She was always worrying about everyone else.

"Why don't you meet me after school, and we'll go to the tryouts together," Blair suggested. "I'm going to need your support."

Frances nodded. "Great. I'll meet you in front of the auditorium at three."

All day Blair had trouble concentrating on her classes. The school was buzzing with talk of the auditions. But finally Blair's last class let out. On the way out of class, she saw Charlie.

He winked at her. "Break a leg!"

"You're not supposed to say that until opening night," Blair protested.

"Well then, break a heart," Charlie joked in return.

I wish I could, thought Blair.

Blair met Frances outside the auditorium. They were both surprised to see how many students were there for the auditions.

"Half the school must be here," Frances whispered as they walked down to the front.

Blair looked around for Shane. She finally spotted him and Margie talking with Mr. Stanley. Blair moved closer to them, pulling Frances along with her. She could see that Margie was very animated, smiling and tossing her hair back over her shoulders. She was wearing a fuzzy low-cut yellow sweater. *She must be freezing in that top*, Blair thought. But she did look more like Juliet than Blair did in her turtleneck. Shane was wearing a white, long-sleeved cotton shirt and a navy vest. He looked like the perfect image of Romeo with his dark, wavy hair and disarming smile. Blair looked at Margie again. Frances watched her gaze as she looked her competition up and down.

"Don't worry, Blair. Just because she looks the part doesn't mean she'll get it."

"I know," said Blair. But she wasn't convinced.

Mr. Stanley called everyone together and asked them to sit in the rows of seats closest to the stage. He talked for a while, telling them how pleased he was to see such a good turnout for the first production of Shakespeare at Pine River High.

"Naturally not all of you will be cast, if only because there aren't enough parts. But we will need people to be in the crowd scenes and chorus, to work on publicity, and on the sets and lighting. I think we can find a job for everyone who's interested."

Then Mr. Stanley passed out the scripts. "Rather than auditioning you in order of the characters' appearance in the play, I am going to ask those of you who are trying out for the smaller roles to go first. That way, those of you who are auditioning for key roles will have a chance to relax into the story. I also want some of you to try out for roles other than the ones you have signed up for. Finally, if you are trying out for several roles, please give each one your best shot."

When the auditions started, Blair kept notes on who she would cast if she could decide. Eric was perfect as even-tempered Benvolio, and Blair was sure he'd get the part. Another boy from the basketball team, Jack Kennon, did well as the feisty Tybalt. He played tough on the court, and he was just as aggressive on the stage. Two boys decided at the last minute to try out for Mercutio, but they weren't nearly as good as Charlie. He really captured the wit and sensitivity of the role.

Finally, Mr. Stanley asked for those who wished

to play Romeo. Shane and two other guys came forward. All of them chose to do Romeo's first long speech at the balcony.

Shane went last and Blair was thrilled to see how convincing he was. He knew the part perfectly, and Blair could hardly wait to act with him. She was sure that Mr. Stanley would have her audition opposite Shane because he was so much better than the others.

After Shane had finished, Mr. Stanley stood up and looked around the auditorium. He nodded at Margie Mason.

"Margie, what scene have you chosen?" he asked.

"The balcony scene, of course," Margie said in a cool voice. She walked up to the stage with confidence. After finding the scene in her script, she called out to Mr. Stanley. "Would it be OK if Shane Lawson read Romeo's lines?" she asked. "We practiced together."

Mr. Stanley shrugged. "Why not? Is that OK with you, Shane?"

"Sure," Shane replied. He walked back onto the stage and smiled at Margie. She said something to him, but Blair couldn't hear what it was. But her smile made Blair furious.

Mr. Stanley instructed Margie to stand on a movable stairway so that she was looking down at Shane. Blair could feel a chill run through her body as she watched them. There was no question that Margie looked like Juliet. Her light sweater emphasized her dark brown hair, which was held back with a clip.

Margie knew the part and didn't make any mistakes. Even Blair had to admit that she was convincing, although her voice didn't carry very well. And with Shane taking Romeo's lines, Blair could see how hard they'd practiced. Their timing was perfect. Blair's heart sank. But she didn't have time to worry. Immediately after they'd finished, Mr. Stanley turned to her.

"Blair, would you go up on the stage? I'd like you to take the nurse's role so that Margie can try another scene."

He looked at Blair's puzzled face and smiled. "I'll ask her to do the same for you."

Shane walked back to his seat while Margie waited, one hand on her hip, for Blair to get in place. She gave Blair a cool smile.

Mr. Stanley jumped up onto the stage and handed Blair a copy of the script. "Here, I want you to do the last part of the Capulet party—the scene where Juliet asks her nurse to find out Romeo's name. Take a few minutes to look over the lines, then you're on."

Blair glanced over the nurse's part. She knew the lines well. She'd had to read them the year before in class, and she liked the dialogue between Juliet and the nurse. And Blair was determined to show Mr. Stanley she was a good actress, that she was good enough to play any part, even though her heart was set on Juliet.

"OK, girls," Mr. Stanley called out. "I'll cue you with Juliet's father's last line." Blair and Margie nodded. " *'I'll do my rest.'* "

Margie stepped forward toward the front of the stage and turned to Blair. She made an impatient gesture with her hand. " *'Come hither, nurse. What is yon gentleman?'* "

Blair bent low, trying to make herself feel like an old woman. Then she said in a cracked but strong voice, " *'The son and heir of old Tiberio.'* "

They continued the scene until the part where Juliet and her nurse are called away. Blair knew they had done very well. In spite of their differences, Blair had to admit that Margie was a fairly good actress.

"Bravo!" said Mr. Stanley. "You were both terrific. Now stay there and reverse the roles. You read Juliet, Blair, and Margie, you read the nurse's lines."

Blair brightened. This was her chance. She smiled at Margie, who suddenly looked bored. Mr. Stanley gave them another few minutes to glance over the script, then cued them.

This time it didn't go well at all. Margie read the nurse's lines in a girl's voice. She made no attempt to capture the age and character of the nurse, and hard as she tried, Blair could not make the scene come alive by herself. When they finished the scene, Blair stared at the floor in frustration. Margie tossed the script onto a chair and left the stage. The auditorium was quiet for a few seconds. Then Mr. Stanley called on one of the boys who had tried out for Romeo.

"'Would you play opposite Blair in the balcony scene please, John?"

Blair looked at Mr. Stanley in dismay. Shane was clearly the best Romeo of the three. Why couldn't Mr. Stanley ask him to play opposite her? She wanted to say something, but the words stuck in her throat. It would be rude to the other boy, and it would also look as if she were unsure of herself. Blair swallowed hard. *I'll do just fine without Shane,* she told herself. *After all, this is only an audition. When I get the part, I'll be playing opposite Shane. That's all that matters.* Blair climbed the stairs with confidence. She had read once that a famous stage actress had said that talent was eighty percent internal inspiration. That had impressed Blair. She knew Juliet's lines, and she knew she'd play them well. Blair looked at John, who was smiling up at her. He had unruly sandy hair, freckles, and to top it off, he was about half her size. He did not look the part of Romeo one bit. *Oh, well,* Blair thought. She took a deep breath.

" *'O Romeo, Romeo! Wherefore art thou Romeo?'* " she began.

Blair looked down at the imaginary garden below her. Suddenly she was distracted by John moving around below so she could see him. And as her mind drifted from thinking about her lines to John's prancing around, her voice faltered. Finally, she reached the cue for Romeo.

Blair waited for John to speak, but he was so busy trying to get her attention that he forgot his one line. Someone could have driven a truck through the pause. When Blair finally hissed at him, he blurted out his line.

Some of the students snickered, and Blair glanced out at them. Her eyes met Margie's, and she could see her critical grin. Blair desperately turned back to her imaginary garden, but she could feel the rush of color in her cheeks. She continued, but she was getting more and more upset by the second. Blair could feel the inspiration draining from her voice—her lines sounded flat and unconvincing. All she could do now was try to get through the scene without bursting into tears.

When she'd finally said her last line, Blair hurried back to her seat. She hunched down in her chair and stared straight ahead. There was an uncomfortable silence, and then Mr. Stanley cleared his throat and stood up.

"I want to thank all of you for coming today. I'll be making my decisions this evening, and I promise to have the cast list posted on the bulletin board across from the drama room by noon tomorrow."

The students filed out of the auditorium, talking among themselves about who they thought should get what part. Blair walked silently beside Frances. She was afraid to say anything for fear her voice would crack. Frances tactfully said nothing. They trudged quietly across the campus until Charlie sprinted up behind them.

"Hey, Blair! You were great!"

Suddenly Blair's self-control collapsed, and she swung around to face Charlie. Tears sprang into her eyes. "Oh, shut up, Charlie. I was horrible and you know it! It was probably the worst audition for Juliet in the history of the theater."

There was a dramatic ring to her last statement, and Charlie's eyes widened. "Maybe, but you were great as the nurse."

Blair closed her eyes to stop the tears. "I don't want to be the nurse," she said slowly. "I want to play *Juliet*."

Charlie backed away, his grin fading. "Well, yeah, I know, but—well, remember what you said to me about playing Mercutio because I was right for the part. . . ." His voice faded away. The look on Blair's face told him he'd blown it, so he threw up his hands. "Well, see you around, Blair—Frances." He turned and dashed off.

Blair blinked back the tears and let out a long sigh of exasperation. Frances wisely said nothing until they reached the corner where she turned off.

" 'Bye, Blair," she said softly. "Don't worry. It'll be OK."

Blair managed a weak smile. "Yeah. Thanks, Frances."

She walked the next few blocks in a daze. It wasn't until she had slammed the door to her bedroom and thrown herself on her bed that she let out her tears.

Chapter Three

Blair barely touched her dinner that night. She picked at her food and only spoke if someone asked her a question. Even then, her answers were short and brief. When Peter loudly asked her about the auditions, she just shrugged and wouldn't look at him. Realizing that something was wrong, Blair's parents left her alone until after dinner, when Blair and her mother were alone in the kitchen.

"What happened, Blair? I can tell that you're upset." Mrs. Young turned from the dishwasher and looked at Blair until she raised her eyes.

"It was awful, Mom. I blew it. I won't get the part." Blair felt the hot sting of tears again.

"What went wrong? Do you want to tell me about it, honey?"

Blair shook her head.

"What scene did you try?" Mrs. Young coaxed.

Reluctantly, Blair told her mother what had happened, first the scenes with Margie, and then the catastrophe with the balcony scene. When she finished, she bit her lip to keep the tears from coming back.

"It sounds like you had a lot going against you," her mother said.

Blair nodded. "It was impossible to do the scene well with Margie playing the nurse. It was like she was trying to make me do badly. I tried to do a good job when *I* was playing the nurse."

"Of course you did, dear. And I'm sure Mr. Stanley knows that. He'll take that into consideration."

"I don't know, Mom. Mr. Stanley knows how much I love to act. It was as if he was testing me—trying to make it harder for me."

"Now, Blair, it's easy to think someone is against you when things go wrong, but that's usually not true. You've had nothing but nice things to say about Mr. Stanley up until now. I know he thinks very highly of you."

"If he thinks so highly of me, why didn't he let me try out with the best Romeo? I think he wants Margie to play Juliet."

"Blair, honey—" Mrs. Young began.

"All right, she was OK. But she wasn't great. And it was so obvious that she was trying to

43

make me look bad. That's not being a good actress *or* a good person."

Blair sighed. She knew getting so upset wouldn't help, but she felt like such a victim. Maybe Mr. Stanley hadn't deliberately tried to make things tough for her, but he sure hadn't made things any easier, either. She glanced at her mother, who was watching her closely. Blair tried to smile.

"That's my girl," said Mrs. Young. "I know you're disappointed, but even if you don't get to play Juliet, it isn't the end of the world. In fact, there was an article about a new summer theater group being formed in Meadowville in the paper today."

Blair's spirits rose slightly. "How far away is Meadowville?"

"It's about thirty-five miles from here, just off the highway to Yosemite."

"That's awfully far."

"Well, you'll be able to get your driver's license right after your birthday," her mother reminded her. "You could take me to work in the morning and take the car to rehearsals. There's a small country road that goes to Meadowville with hardly any traffic, so you could avoid the highway. Besides," she added, "there will probably be other people from Pine River in the play. You can car-pool with them."

Blair knew her mother was trying to soften the day's disappointment, but summer seemed like such a long way off. And the thought of having to watch Margie Mason play Juliet still made her furious.

"I'm sorry I'm acting like such a spoiled brat, Mom, but I really wanted that part," said Blair.

"I know you did, dear, and you would have done a good job. But you're still very young; there will be other plays."

"I know, but . . ." Blair's voice trailed off.

Her mother patted her cheek gently. "Listen, honey, there's something else I wanted to talk to you about. I'm not sure if you heard, but Bill Olsen twisted his ankle in practice today. He may not be able to play Saturday, and Dad's very concerned. I think he'd appreciate it if we try to be extra thoughtful; he's under a lot of pressure."

Bill Olsen was a senior and the first-string center on the basketball team. Blair knew he scored a lot of points for the team. She suddenly felt guilty for being so involved in her own problems.

"Do you think Dad will use Charlie?"

"He'll have to if Bill can't play."

"Well, if Charlie is as good at basketball as he is at Shakespeare, they'll win for sure!"

"Let's keep our fingers crossed." Mrs. Young

paused for a minute. Then she said, "Listen, honey. Why don't we go downtown tomorrow night and go clothes shopping. We haven't done that in a while, and the stores will be open late."

"Only if you get something new, too," Blair replied.

Her mother smiled. "OK. You've got a deal."

By the time Blair and Frances reached school the next morning, Blair was in a bad mood again. She dreaded having to go look at the cast list.

"I'll just wait in the cafeteria," Blair said to Frances. "You can tell me who got what."

"Oh, no!" Frances protested. "You're coming with me. Don't let Margie have the satisfaction of seeing you disappointed. No matter what happens, you've got to look like it doesn't bother you."

Blair looked at Frances in surprise. Her quiet, unassuming friend always amazed Blair with her good sense. And Blair knew that Frances was right. She would go—but it was going to be very difficult to look at Margie's name next to *Juliet* when she had counted on seeing her own there.

The morning dragged on, and everyone seemed to be waiting anxiously for the cast list to be posted. It was hard for Blair not to worry that everyone was talking about how badly she'd done at the audition, but she knew in her heart that it wasn't true. She didn't feel that way about the other people who had tried out and not done well. She suddenly realized how easy it was to become preoccupied with your own mistakes and disappointments.

When the lunch bell finally rang, Blair dragged herself from her geometry class to meet Frances and walk to the drama room with her.

"Well, Fran, at least you'll get the part of the nurse," Blair said when she met her friend. "Those other girls acted much too young."

"I wasn't much better," said Frances. "I wish I had decided sooner so I could have had you coach me. You do character roles so well."

But not the romantic ones, thought Blair.

The cast list was up, and a mob of students was gathered around it. Some of them were smiling, others were obviously disappointed. No one said much for fear the person next to him or her hadn't been cast.

"Come on," said Frances, pushing her way into the crowd and pulling Blair by the arm. When they were in front of the list, Blair tried to focus her eyes on the names but they were a blur. Her heart was beating hard, and she tried to breathe deeply and read the names.

"Pam and Laura got the parts they wanted," Frances announced, realizing that Blair wasn't concentrating. "And so did Shane and Charlie. And Eric got Benvolio." Finally Blair began to read the list. The first name she read was Margie's opposite Juliet. Blair turned away and threaded her way through the group of kids. Just as she reached the edge of the crowd, she came face-to-face with Margie, who smiled confidently.

"Well," Margie began in a cool, challenging tone.

"Congratulations," said Blair quietly and pushed past her. When she reached the end of the hallway, Frances caught up with her.

"Blair," she panted, "you're the nurse."

Blair stared at her in disbelief. "What? But I don't—but Frances, you wanted to be the nurse."

Frances smiled. It was a genuine smile, and Blair suddenly felt terrible. She was feeling sorry for herself because she hadn't gotten the part she wanted, but she hadn't thought to feel sorry that she *had* gotten the part her best friend wanted.

"I'm not going to take it, Fran," Blair said suddenly. "Don' t worry! You wanted the part, and you should get it. You were good!" she said firmly. "I'm going—"

"Blair," Frances interrupted. "You played the

nurse much better than I did. And the parts should go to the people who play them the best, not the ones who want them the most. Besides"—she smiled—"I'm the understudy for both the nurse and Juliet."

"Both roles?" asked Blair.

"I guess Mr. Stanley figured you and Margie won't get sick at the same time," she said with a laugh. Suddenly Frances looked very excited. "You know what else, Blair? You're the assistant director."

"What?" Blair was stunned. "Assistant director? Me?"

"You know the play better than anyone except maybe Charlie," said Frances. "And I think—I think Mr. Stanley wants you to learn about directing."

Blair's mind was reeling. Now she had a part and she was going to help direct, too. Blair didn't know whether to laugh or to cry. She looked at Frances helplessly. *Why is Mr. Stanley doing this?* Blair wondered. She felt overwhelmed. "Oh, brother," Blair finally said weakly.

"I told you it would all work out," said Frances.

"You sound like my mother!" Blair joked. They both laughed.

As they were talking, Blair noticed Shane out of the corner of her eye. He walked over to them and spoke to Blair.

"Hey, congratulations. You were terrific as the nurse. And I still think you would have been a great Juliet."

Blair shrugged, even though she was thrilled by Shane's compliment. "But Margie was much better." She wondered if she would be struck dead for such a lie.

Shane frowned. "Don't sell yourself short, Blair. You're a talented actress." He turned to leave. "I've got to go now. See you guys later."

" 'Bye, Shane," both girls chorused.

Frances looked at Blair and winked. "See, he wants you to play Juliet."

Blair said nothing, but inside she was ecstatic.

The girls headed toward the cafeteria, and on the way they ran into Charlie. He looked at Blair hesitantly, remembering their uncomfortable encounter after the auditions. Blair knew she should try to make up for being so rude.

"Hi, Charlie," she said in a cheerful voice. "Congratulations!"

"Thanks—uh, same to you," he said, watching her expression.

Blair smiled. "I'm sorry I was such a rat yesterday. I was just disappointed with myself."

"That's OK, Blair," said Charlie. "I guess I wasn't very tactful, but you were really great playing the nurse. And I know that scene with Margie wasn't your fault."

"Thanks, Charlie, but—I just didn't do very well, that's all."

"Well, as far as I'm concerned, Blair, you were perfect as Juliet when we were practicing. And I'll always think of you as Juliet."

He spoke so fervently that both Blair and Frances laughed. Blair thought how sweet it was of Charlie to try to make her feel better.

"Listen, you guys," Frances said once they'd gotten through the cafeteria line, "I'm going to take my lunch and sit in the corner. I've got a Spanish exam next period, and I want to look over my notes."

"OK, Fran," said Blair. "Good luck."

"Do you mind if I eat lunch with you, Blair?" Charlie asked.

"No," she answered. "Let's go find a place near the window."

They walked over to an empty table and sat down. Charlie propped his feet up on the chair next to him and proceded to spread out two bologna sandwiches, two containers of milk, and a huge piece of chocolate cake. Blair looked at him in amusement.

"You eat more than I do, Charlie! And that's saying something."

"This?" said Charlie with mock surprise. "This is just a small snack."

"Well, I guess you're going to need all that

food. My dad said this morning that you are going to have to play the whole game tomorrow if Bill's ankle doesn't get better."

"I know," Charlie replied, his tone growing serious. "And I know how much winning this game means to your dad, and to the whole team. I hope I don't disappoint everyone."

"You won't," said Blair firmly. "My dad thinks you're one of the best centers he's ever seen. I overheard him telling Peter that after a game a few weeks ago."

Charlie's face lit up with pride. "He really said that? Honest?" Blair nodded, and he settled back in his chair, staring off into space. Then he sat up abruptly. "I really love basketball. It's such a complete sport. I mean, you need strength, speed, grace . . . And when things go just right—when you make that impossible basket"—he shook his head—"there's nothing like it."

Blair was surprised to hear Charlie sound so poetic. He joked so much that she'd thought he wasn't serious about anything. But she realized then that underneath the clown act he was a very sensitive person.

While Blair was thinking about Charlie, he was studying her. "You know, Blair, I really think you're great." His words came out slowly. "I mean—since we've been in class together . . . And I really thought you'd get the part of Juliet. When things didn't go right for you I felt terrible. It was a tough break, but you just have to forget about it." Blair looked at him, half expecting a lecture on accepting disappointment.

"But I really meant what I said yesterday," he continued. "You were great as the nurse—better than anyone else." Blair started to interrupt him, but he put her off. "No, wait, Blair. The nurse is a hard role! She's a pivotal character, and it takes talent to play that kind of part. You've got that talent. That's one of the reasons I'm glad I'm in this play—because I'll be working with you."

Charlie's words made Blair blush. She knew he was trying to make her feel better, but she could also tell that he'd meant what he said and she was flattered. After lunch, Blair walked away thinking that Charlie McGuire was one of the kindest people she knew. She was glad they were becoming friends. Now all she had to do was get to know Shane Lawson better, too. One of the reasons she had wanted so badly to play Juliet was so she could get closer to him. *Well, she reasoned, at least I'm in the play. And I'm going to help direct. Maybe I'll even get to direct Shane—in a performance meant for only two.*

After school, the cast for *Romeo and Juliet* met in Mr. Stanley's classroom to discuss the rehearsal schedule. Blair spotted the empty seat next to Shane and grabbed it. He smiled at her, and her heart flew up to her throat.

"Hi, Blair. All ready to start rehearsals?"

"Well," Blair said, "you know playing the nurse wasn't my first choice, but yes, I guess I'm ready." She gave a short laugh.

"Yes, Blair. It's perfect casting. Congratulations." Margie had come up behind Blair and had heard her comment to Shane. She sat down on the other side of him and leaned across his desk toward Blair. Her smile was patronizing. "I know you wanted Juliet, but you'll be much better as the nurse."

Blair's cheeks flamed at Margie's snide comment. She was grateful when Mr. Stanley called the class to order.

"By now all of you have seen the cast list. I hope none of you are too disappointed." He looked around the room, and Blair was convinced that his eyes stayed on her the longest. Then he went on. "As you know, Blair Young will be helping me direct. Blair has a lot of acting ability and interest in the theater. I thought it would be good to have her broaden that interest. Also"—he smiled at Blair—"she knows the play incredibly well."

Mr. Stanley paced in front of his desk. "It's helpful, too, to have someone assisting me who is onstage part of the time. That person can get a different perspective of the blocking." He paused, and someone raised a hand.

"Excuse me, Mr. Stanley." It was one of the girls who was going to be in the chorus. "What does blocking mean?"

"It's the actors' placement and movements onstage," Mr. Stanley explained. "Proper blocking is very important for the acoustics as well as for the action of a performance."

"When do rehearsals start?" someone else asked.

"We'll start next Monday, right after the last class of the day," answered Mr. Stanley. "Next week will be a little frantic, and we'll just be reading the play to get the story down. And because several members of the basketball team have major roles, Coach Young has agreed to hold his practice at five o'clock next week. As you know, the semifinal game is tomorrow and if they win, they'll go to the finals next Saturday. I hope everyone will come out and support the team."

Everyone looked around the room, smiling at the team members. Out of the corner of her eye, Blair saw Margie reach over and squeeze Shane's hand. She wished she dared to do something like that.

"But if we don't win," Charlie said lightly, "you're off the hook for the following Saturday."

"You'll win!" said Blair firmly.

"She has to say that," Charlie kidded. Everyone laughed.

When the laughter died down, Mr. Stanley talked about the necessity of understanding the play as soon as possible.

"I'm happy to say that my drama class knows this play pretty well. If any of you who are not in my class have any trouble understanding your lines, be sure to ask my drama students, especially"—he nodded at Blair and Charlie—"the assistant director and Mercutio. They should be able to help."

Later, as they left the class, Blair fell into step next to Shane. Charlie and Eric were a few steps behind them. As they started across the campus, Margie appeared on the other side of Shane. Blair wanted to tell her to get lost, but she was silent. Margie looked up at Shane and smiled.

"Hi, Romeo," she said sweetly.

Shane mumbled something, and Charlie and Eric started to rib him.

" '*Wherefore art thou, darling Romeo,*' " said Charlie in a high-pitched voice.

" '*O, speak again, bright angel!*' " teased Eric,

ruffling Shane's hair. Shane turned and took a couple of playful swings at both of them.

Just then Frances came running up to Blair. "Blair, I can't walk home with you today. I've got to go to the library and finish my history report."

"Sure, Fran," said Blair. "I'll call you tonight, OK?"

Frances nodded and hurried off, but not before Blair saw her look briefly at Eric.

When Frances was out of earshot, Margie said in a pitying tone, "Poor Frances, she's so shy. I guess that's why she studies so hard."

"Don't be sorry, Margie," said Blair in Frances's defense. "She works hard, but she's also a good friend and a lot of fun." *Unlike you,* Blair wanted to add.

There was silence. Then Eric nodded. "Blair's right. Frances is really nice."

Blair couldn't wait to tell Frances what Eric had said. She'd be thrilled.

"And she sure helped me get through algebra freshman year. I was lost," said Charlie.

"Me, too," echoed Shane. "She's helped all of us all through one class or another."

So there, thought Blair, looking at Margie out of the corner of her eye. But Margie looked just as smug as ever. She put her hand on Shane's arm and pulled him off toward the gym.

"Come on, Shane. I'll walk you to practice."

"OK," Shane agreed. "Are you guys coming?"

Eric nodded, but Charlie said, "You go ahead. I'll be right there. I want to tell Blair something."

Charlie walked beside Blair while the others headed off toward the gym. Blair looked over her shoulder to see Margie cuddling up to Shane. When she turned back to Charlie, she was scowling.

Charlie grinned. "I know it's hard to compete with Margie's act, Blair, but don't worry. She's been after Shane since they were in kindergarten. Until now, he never looked at her twice."

Blair tightened her mouth. "I'm not interested in competing with Margie Mason, Charlie. Look where it got me with Juliet."

"Oh, that doesn't count." He paused. "What I mean is, you're both so different that I hate to see you fighting over Shane."

Blair looked at him indignantly. "Oh, really?"

"There I go again." Charlie let out a sigh. "What I mean, Blair, is that Margie's one of those girls who attracts guys and . . ."

"So what am I," asked Blair in an icy tone, "chopped liver?"

She had heard someone use that expression once and had been dying to use it. But it sounded so funny when she said it that she broke up laughing. Charlie laughed, too.

"Sorry, Blair, I'm always sticking my foot in my mouth with you. I guess I'd better go before I say something wrong again. Besides, I've got to get to practice or your dad will kill me. Anyway, I just wanted to tell you that I thought it was nice how you stuck up for Frances."

"Frances is a very good person," said Blair, stiffly. "And she's my best friend."

"I know." Charlie grinned. "Stay on my side, too, will you?" And he dashed off to the gym.

Blair watched him go and shook her head. But there was a happy smile on her face.

That evening, Blair and her mother ate early so they could go shopping. Peter decided to wait to eat until their father came home from practice, so while Mrs. Young went to change her uniform, Blair explained to Peter what to do about dinner. "And don't forget to be extra nice to Dad, OK?"

"I *am* nice. I'm *always* nice. You're the yo-yo in this family!"

"What's that supposed to mean?" Blair cried.

"You're happy as can be one day and then a big grump the next, that's what!" Peter explained in a loud voice.

Later, when they were in the car, Blair looked at her mother. "Have I really been acting awful lately?" she asked as they started off for the new shopping mall nearby. "Peter says I'm moody. Well, he didn't exactly say it that way—you know how he talks."

Blair's mother smiled. "I think I understand how you've been feeling—we all have our ups and downs. And high school can be very hard, maybe more so for girls than boys. Peter will have his share in time."

"You should be a psychiatrist, Mom," said Blair. "You understand things so well."

"Actually, I considered becoming a psychiatrist after my second year of nursing school."

"Why didn't you?" Blair asked, curious.

"Because I decided to marry your dad instead."

Blair grinned. "I think you made the right decision."

Chapter Four

As Blair came downstairs the next morning, she heard her parents talking in the kitchen.

"Then he's definitely out?" Mrs. Young asked.

"I'm afraid so. I really don't see how I can use him. He was still limping badly yesterday."

"Bill can't play, huh?" Blair could see the concern on her mother's face.

"*He* says he can, but Dr. Olsen checked Bill's ankle again this morning, and it doesn't look good. I trust his opinion, even if it's mixed with a little fatherly caution."

"I'd certainly take his advice. He's a good doctor," said Mrs. Young.

Blair went to the refrigerator and took out the orange juice. She poured herself a glass and sat down across from her father, who was toying absently with his coffee cup.

"You know, Dad, I'm convinced Charlie can play the whole game—and win, too. We all know he has a lot of energy, but in the last week I've realized how much determination he has. Look at how hard he worked to understand Shakespeare. He already knows practically all his lines. I think you should just let him know that you have faith in him."

Mr. Young smiled at his daughter. "You're pretty smart, Blair. I *will* tell him. And I agree with you about his energy level. He's hardly ever tired, even after a long practice." Mr. Young stood up. "You'll be there to help cheer us on, won't you?"

"You bet! I've even got a new outfit to wear."

"Can I go with you and Frances, Blair?" Peter had walked in on the last of their conversation. "Mom has to work until three, so she's going to be late, and Benny's sick."

Benny was Peter's best friend, and he usually went to the games with the Young family. Blair glanced at her mother, who shook her head and shrugged.

"I'm sorry, Blair, but I have to work today. We have a lot of nurses out with the flu—"

"That's what Benny has," Peter interrupted.

"Do you mind if Peter goes with you and Fran, honey? He can come back with me afterward."

Blair was not pleased, but she knew better

than to make a fuss. Her father had a lot on his mind, and her mother was working too much overtime as it was.

"'Yeah, it's OK," Blair said, trying to smile. She turned to Peter. "I'm leaving to meet Fran at one-thirty, Peter, so be ready!"

Peter nodded.

"Thanks, honey," said Mrs. Young. She gave Blair a peck on the cheek and left the room to get ready for work.

Mr. Young took a final gulp of coffee and took his jacket off the back of his chair. "Well, I guess I'd better get over to the gym."

"Why are you leaving so early?" Blair asked. "The game's not for hours."

"I told the boys I'd take them out for breakfast, but I don't want them to eat too close to the game. It'll also give me a chance to gear Charlie up with a good pep talk."

Around noon, Blair took a shower and washed her hair. She tried to blow it dry in the same soft style she had seen on a model in *Seventeen* magazine, but she didn't have much luck. Finally, she pulled it back with some new combs her mother had bought for her. The style made her face look a little thin, but she did look more sophisticated.

Blair then went to her closet and took out the new corduroy jumper she and her mother had bought the night before. It was a deep green, with a scoop neck and a dropped waist. The skirt had soft pleats that skimmed her hips and fell to just below her knees. She chose a rose-colored turtleneck to go under the jumper and decided to wear boots for a very wintery effect. She wondered briefly if Shane would notice. Then she realized she was being stupid. Shane would have other things on his mind.

By the time Blair walked back downstairs, Peter was waiting for her in the kitchen.

"I'm ready," he said impatiently.

"I'll call Fran's house and see if she's left yet," said Blair, wishing she and Frances could go to the game alone.

Frances's mother said she had just left, so Blair put on her quilted jacket, and she and Peter set off for the corner to meet Fran. She was waiting when they got there.

Frances blew on her hands as they quickly headed for the school gym. "Boy, am I glad basketball is an indoor sport."

"So am I," Blair agreed. She pulled Peter by the arm. "Come on, Peter. It's cold."

"What about Bill. Is his ankle better?" Frances asked.

Blair shook her head. "Charlie has to play the entire game."

"Charlie's really good," Peter panted, trying to

keep up with the two girls. "He'll win the game for us."

Blair had learned to enjoy basketball over the past season, and she truly hoped the Pine River team would win today. She was also wondering if there was going to be a victory party if they did win.

"Did you hear about any parties after the game?" Blair said to Frances in a low voice.

"What?" said Peter. "I can't hear you."

"I'm not talking to you!" Blair said in an irritated voice.

"You're talking about a party, aren't you?" he persisted.

"If you heard, why did you ask?" Blair snapped, trying not to lose her patience. "It's none of your business anyway, Peter."

"Well, I haven't heard anyone asking you to a party, either!" Peter retorted.

Blair didn't answer, but Frances added quietly, "I'll bet Charlie will ask you to go if they win."

"But, I—" Blair didn't finish. She wanted to say that she didn't want Charlie to ask her. She wanted to go with Shane. But she didn't even dare to tell Frances how she felt, and she certainly didn't want to give Peter anything to talk about.

"If Charlie asks you, can I go, too?" Peter asked.

"Peter!" Blair's voice was exasperated.

"It's a high school party, Peter." Frances spoke softly. She was always so patient with Peter.

Peter accepted her explanation with a shrug.

They finally arrived at the door to the gym, and the crowds were filing in. Blair went first, leading Peter and Frances to a front bleacher. They had come early enough to be able to sit directly behind the Pine River team. The boys were still in the locker room, but the cheerleaders for both sides were warming up. Blair looked at Margie Mason in her bright blue pleated skirt and white sweater, the Pine River High colors. Margie had tied her hair back in a ponytail to look like the other girls, but Blair had to admit that she stood out. She was prettier than the others and just as good, if not better than, the senior cheerleaders.

Blair looked over to the other side of the gym. Pine River's opposition was Meadowville High School. Meadowville was also a small town, but they had always had the best athletic teams in the league. Blair knew that her father felt they were tough competition.

A few minutes before the game began, the teams ran out to their respective benches. Blair was thrilled when Shane sat right in front of her. Charlie was next to him, and when he turned to wave at her, Shane turned, too, and smiled. Blair could feel her heart quicken, and she gave them both a victory sign.

"I think Shane was smiling at you, Bean," Peter said. "Please don't faint on the floor, it will embarrass me."

"Peter!" Blair hissed.

"Hey, Frances." Peter leaned across Blair to get Frances's attention. "Did you know that when basketball was first invented they used a regular old basket with a bottom in it? Every time anybody scored, someone had to climb up a ladder and get the ball out."

Blair looked skeptically at Peter. "Who told you that?"

"Charlie did. I was talking to him after one of the games. He knows all sorts of neat stuff!"

Blair said nothing. She looked across the gym to see the Meadowville rooting section spell out "Bulldogs." In return, Pine River's rooting section flashed "Wildcats," and a big cheer rose up from the stands. The cheerleaders ran out on the floor for one more routine before the players were introduced. Blair tried not to look at Margie, but she did watch Shane to see if he was looking at her. She was relieved to see he was talking to Charlie and another forward instead.

The Bulldogs were introduced first. After each

name was called, Meadowville let out a support-ive cheer. They stood in a line as the Pine River team repeated the introduction process. Then each player took a few steps forward to shake the hand of a member of the opposing team. To make up for Bill Olsen's absence, Charlie shook hands with two players on the Meadowville team, crossing his arms awkwardly. It was a comical gesture, and everyone laughed. *Trust Charlie to start everything off with a laugh*, Blair thought.

The starting lineup fell into position while the others ran off the court. The referee, a whis-tle between his teeth, stood at the center circle. He held the ball in his hands while Charlie and the opposing center eyed it closely.

"All set?" he yelled. Silence filled the gym. The players were all standing absolutely still, ready to spring into action at a second's notice.

The referee blew his whistle and tossed the ball into the air. Charlie shot up and tapped the ball to Shane, who turned and charged down the court, scoring easily. But Meadowville quickly came back with a basket of their own.

The first two quarters continued at the same pace, each team trading off a score. Shane made the most points for the Wildcats, but Charlie was working hard, too. Blair had heard her father tell him to pace himself since he was going to play the whole game, but she could see by half time that he was winded.

During the break, the band played, and the cheerleaders ran out on the floor to root for their respective schools. Blair watched Margie for a while, then her eyes traveled back to Shane. He looked tired, too, and the entire team seemed tense. The score was tied at 38, and Blair realized they were going to be under even more pressure during the second half. Blair thought of Charlie. She knew that her dad would give Shane a break, but Charlie wouldn't get any rest.

When the Wildcats' cheerleaders came back to sit down, Blair saw Margie Mason walk up behind Shane. She tapped him gently on the shoulder and he turned around. It made Blair angry to see them smile at each other. Why couldn't she go up to Shane like that? She was sitting only a few feet from him.

"Hey, Bean, someone's stealing your boyfriend," Peter teased.

"Huh?" answered Blair vaguely.

"M-A-R-G-I-E M-A-S-O-N," Peter spelled loudly. Fortunately Mrs. Young arrived before Blair could strangle him.

"Tied, huh?" she said, sitting between her son and daughter, much to Blair's relief.

"Yeah, it's been a good game," replied Blair.

"Shane's been doing most of the scoring, but Charlie's playing a cool, steady game."

"I'll bet he's going to be tired tonight," said Mrs. Young, sympathetically.

"If you ask me," said Peter, leaning across his mother to look at Blair, "Charlie's a much better player than Shane."

"No one asked you," Blair snapped back.

Just then, the whistle blew and the players were on the floor in seconds. Mr. Young had pulled Shane out for the quarter, along with both of the original guards. Blair could see the Bulldogs had a whole new lineup, including a new center. Charlie looked over at the bench and for a second, Blair thought he looked worried. She raised her hand in a fist and smiled at him just as their eyes met. He grinned and suddenly looked alive again.

As if Blair's signal had inspired him, Charlie was all over the court, scoring like the best sharpshooter in the league. Usually Charlie was a team player, but without Shane he seemed to play for both of them. Blair's father stood nervously on the sidelines, occasionally glancing down to see that his feet didn't step over into the court. A few fouls had been called on both teams in the first half, but during the third quarter, the Bulldogs made more than their share of mistakes. And each time they failed,

Charlie scored on free throws. It was as if his lightning style had unnerved the Bulldogs. By the end of the third quarter, the score was 66–58 in favor of the Wildcats.

In the brief minute between the third and fourth quarters, Charlie ran back to the bench to mop himself off.

"Take it easy, Charlie," Blair heard her father say. "Let Shane do the work. You've turned the game around!"

"But I'm on a roll," Charlie protested with a laugh. He did exactly as he was told, though, and Shane went into action, faster than he had been in the first half. Within minutes, the score was 78–68 in favor of Pine River.

Neither team scored for several minutes. Then, in the last few seconds of the game, Charlie came to Shane's aid. The ball had been passed to Shane by the other Pine River forward. But for some reason, the ball slipped from Shane's grasp. Charlie, who was within two feet of him, swooped up the ball and spun around. He hooked a shot into the basket just as the whistle blew. The final score was Pine River 80, Meadowville 68.

The home crowd went wild! Briefly, Blair looked over at the Bulldog section and felt sorry for them. But as soon as she saw Charlie and Shane being carried off the court on the shoulders of their teammates, she, too, jumped up and joined the cheering. Peter dashed out and stood, awed, in front of Charlie and Shane. Charlie jumped down and shook Peter's hand. He grinned.

"We did it, huh?"

"You were great, Charlie," Peter said breathlessly. "Just great!"

Blair and Frances waited while the band played and the cheerleaders performed a final tribute to the team. The Meadowville team gave a cheer for their opponents, but Blair could see their hearts weren't in it. She knew how disappointed they must feel, having gotten so close to the title. Pine River was now league winner, and in a week they would play the champions of the other league in the area. Blair felt a rush of pride in her father.

When the team left for the locker room, Blair and Frances started to leave. Peter was going to ride home with Mrs. Young, and Blair was glad that she and Frances would have a chance to talk about the game without her brother's wisecracks. Just as they got to the door, Blair heard someone call her name. She turned and saw Bill Olsen limping toward her. She had never spoken to him before, but she knew who he was.

"Hi, Bill. Great game, huh?"

"Terrific, except I hate to see how well they do without me." He gave a short laugh. Blair knew how hard it must have been for Bill to miss playing in such an important game.

"I think everyone worked extra hard to make up for you being out."

Bill smiled. "Thanks. Listen, Blair, there's a party tonight at my house—it's the least I can do for the team. Would you like to come?" He looked over at Frances and said hurriedly, "You, too, uh—?"

"Frances Barker," said Blair, "this is Bill Olsen." She felt funny introducing someone she had never really met.

"Nice to meet you, Frances," Bill replied.

"Thanks for inviting us. We'd love to come." She glanced over at Frances, who smiled and nodded.

"Okay. See you about seven-thirty!" He smiled again and limped away.

When they got outside, Blair turned to Frances. "I'll bet Eric will be there, Fran."

"So will Shane," she responded with a grin.

Blair frowned. "And so will Margie."

Shortly after Blair got home, the phone rang. Peter answered it and yelled for Blair. "It's for you, Bean. It's Charlie!"

Blair picked up the phone, wishing it wasn't Charlie, but Shane.

"Hi, Charlie. Congratulations. You were terrific!"

"Thanks, Blair. And thanks for cheering us on. Listen, Blair, I can't talk long—I'm at the pay phone by the gym and your dad wants to talk to us some more. Anyway, I was just wondering if you'd like to go—uh—if you'd like a ride to Bill's party tonight? He told me he invited you."

Blair hesitated. Was Charlie asking her for a date? She did like him, but she wasn't sure she wanted to go on a real *date* with him.

"Frances could come, too," Charlie offered. "Bill said he invited you both, and we can all go together. I'm sure my dad will give me the car tonight." Blair could hear the pride in his voice and she smiled into the phone.

"Sure, Charlie, that would be great. What time?"

"Is seven-fifteen OK?"

"Perfect. See you then."

" 'Bye, Blair."

Blair immediately dialed Frances's number and told her what Charlie had said.

"But, Blair," she protested, "I don't want to butt in on a date."

"It's not a date," Blair assured her friend. "

don't want it to look like I'm Charlie's date, and I want you to come along."

Frances paused. "Well, all right. But I know Charlie likes you, and I'm sure he'd prefer it if I didn't tag along."

Blair hung up a few minutes later and walked into the kitchen. Her mother was standing by the counter seasoning steaks for dinner, looking relaxed and happy.

"I certainly think it was a good idea to move here," Blair said, breaking up the lettuce for the salad.

"I'm glad you've grown to like it, dear. Your father and I certainly do."

"Boy, is he going to be in a good mood tonight." Blair chuckled and her mother laughed aloud. *She looks so young,* Blair thought as she watched her mother push a strand of hair out of her face. Both of her parents were so understanding, especially compared to Frances's. Frances was the youngest child in a large family, and it seemed as if her mother and father had gotten tired of being parents by the time Frances was born. Blair looked at her mother again.

"Could I invite Frances to dinner? I know she would love to come, and she can share my steak."

"That's a lovely idea, Blair. And don't worry, we have plenty of meat."

A half hour later, Frances was at the kitchen door with a loaf of fresh-baked bread from the nearby bakery.

"How thoughtful of you, Frances. Thank you."

"You're welcome, Mrs. Young. Thank *you* for inviting me."

A little before six, Blair's father came home. He looked tired but happy. He hugged them all, including Frances, and they all sat down in the living room, talking about the game beside the warmth of a crackling fire.

"Charlie really came through today," said Mr. Young. "He was still full of energy when we got back to the locker room."

"See, Dad, I told you," Blair said.

"I can't believe it," Mrs. Young added. "Remember that game you played against Stanford, Bud? You had to play three quarters because everyone was fouling out?"

Mr. Young grinned and nodded.

Blair's mother turned to the girls. "We went to a victory dinner that night, and the star center fell asleep. He just pushed his plate back and put his head on his arms."

They were all sitting around the dinner table laughing when Charlie arrived an hour and a half later. Mr. Young rose from his chair and shook Charlie's hand.

"I'm so proud of you, Charlie," he said warmly.

"I'm proud of all my players, but you and Shane saved the day."

"Thanks, Coach. I'm pretty proud of myself—and Shane, too, of course." He winked at Blair, and she could feel the color rising in her cheeks.

"I saw your parents at the game, Charlie," said Mrs. Young. "I'll bet they're very happy tonight."

"They sure are." Charlie grinned. "My mom made me fried chicken and lemon meringue pie—my favorites—for a victory dinner."

"What would she have done if you'd lost?" Peter asked innocently.

"Given it to the dog, I guess," Charlie quipped. They laughed, and Charlie looked at Blair and Frances.

"Ready, ladies?"

The girls nodded and stood up. Charlie gave Peter a pat on the back, and he and the girls walked out to his car.

Bill Olsen lived on the other side of town, in a new, split-level house with a huge family room. When they walked in, the stereo was blasting and a few kids were dancing. But most people were standing around talking about the game. Blair looked to see if Shane was there yet. He wasn't. Charlie found Dr. Olsen, Bill's father, who had come in to compliment the team on their victory. Blair's mother worked with Dr. Olsen at the hospital.

"I know your mother, Blair. She's a fine nurse. And today I must say that your father is one fine coach. I'm just sorry Bill wasn't able to play."

"Me, too," Blair replied. "And I know Dad was very disappointed when Bill hurt his ankle."

Just then, Shane walked in with Margie hanging on his arm. Blair could feel herself stiffen almost involuntarily. The other kids cheered and Charlie walked up to Shane and slapped him on the back.

"I thought you might have fallen asleep already."

"Who, me?" Shane grinned and Margie laughed. Then she glanced over at Blair.

"Oh, look—the coach's daughter is here." Her tone was mocking, and Blair looked away.

"Hi, Blair," said Shane, pulling away from Margie. He walked over to her. "I'm glad you're here."

Blair blinked. Shane had actually left Margie and come over to talk to her! She tried to think of something witty to say. Fortunately, Frances, who was standing next to her, complimented Shane on the game, giving Blair time to compose herself.

"My father's very proud of you," Blair finally said.

Shane's eyes lit up. "Really? He did look pretty happy after the game. But I know he was really nervous before." Shane laughed, and Blair thought for the millionth time what a beautiful smile he had.

"He said you and Charlie saved the day," Blair went on. She wished she could think of something besides what her father had to say, but her mind had suddenly turned to Jell-O.

"Hey, Shane, let's dance." Margie had walked over and was tugging on Shane's arm. He looked at her, then back at Blair. He shrugged. "OK. See you later, Blair."

"Margie's pretty aggressive," said Frances after they'd left.

"I'll say," Blair replied in an irritated tone.

The next song came on, and Margie was still holding on to Shane. Charlie came over to Blair. "Want to dance?"

Blair looked at him and then at Shane and Margie. She shrugged. "Sure. Why not?"

Charlie was a surprisingly good dancer. In spite of his long legs, he was incredibly light on his feet. In fact, he was probably the best dancer in the room. Blair was pretty good herself and when the music stopped, everyone was looking at them. To her surprise, Shane walked away from Margie and cut in on Charlie.

"You don't mind if I dance with Blair, do you, man?" he said to Charlie.

Charlie shrugged. "Nah. I should probably spread myself around—give all the girls a chance to dance with the Fred Astaire of Pine River." He walked over to Frances, who was sitting by herself on the couch. "Come on, Fran, you're the next lucky lady." Frances giggled and got up to dance with him, but this time the music was slow. Shane took Blair in his arms, and they danced so closely that she was afraid he could feel her heart beating. She couldn't think of anything to say, but it didn't matter; Shane didn't say anything either. Blair felt as if she were going to faint from happiness, and she closed her eyes. She only opened them once during the dance, just in time to see Margie scowl at her.

When the music stopped, Shane didn't let go of her. He just smiled and didn't say anything until the music started up again. This time the beat was fast, and they broke apart. Blair had to admit that Charlie was a better dancer than Shane, but she was so happy to be with Shane that she didn't care. When the song was over, they were both out of breath.

"Hang on, Blair. I'll go get us both a Coke."

Shane disappeared, and seconds later Margie was at Blair's side.

"In case you didn't realize it, Coach's Daughter," she said icily, "Shane is *my* date."

Blair stared at her. She was about to say something, but just then Shane arrived with two Cokes. Margie reached out for one of them.

"Thank you, Shane."

"But—"

"Never mind, Shane. I'm not really thirsty," Blair said calmly. But inside she was furious. "I think I'll go over and sit with Frances for a while." She smiled at Shane. "Thanks for the dance."

Blair walked away quickly and went to sit with Charlie and Frances. They were talking about the upcoming rehearsals for *Romeo and Juliet*. She forced herself to look involved in their conversation, but in her mind, she was still thinking about Margie's comment. How dare she act so possessive! After all, *Shane* had asked *her* to dance.

Blair stuck close to Frances and Charlie for the rest of the evening. She and Charlie danced a couple of times, and she tried to tell herself to just be happy that she'd gotten to dance with Shane at all. *It's a beginning,* she told herself.

The party broke up around eleven since most of the boys there were on the team, and they were pretty tired. Shane came up to Blair to say good-bye while Margie waited impatiently by the door.

"See you at school, Blair."

" 'Bye, Shane."

When Blair got into the car with Charlie and Frances, she was very quiet. She kept thinking about dancing with Shane and how nice his arms had felt around her. If only Margie weren't so darned pushy, she thought. The three drove in silence for a few blocks, then Frances asked Charlie to take her home first. Blair didn't particularly want to be alone with him, but it made sense since she lived closer to Charlie's house than Frances did. After they dropped Frances off, Charlie glanced over at Blair.

"You sure are quiet tonight."

"I guess I'm tired, Charlie." She managed to laugh a little. "You don't know how much energy we use just cheering for you guys."

Charlie didn't say anything, but when she opened the door to get out, he said, "Blair, listen—" he paused.

She turned to look at him. "Yes, Charlie?"

"Take it easy, will you?"

"I don't know what you mean." She tried to sound nonchalant.

"I think you do, Blair. Look, I just don't like to see you get caught in the middle of something." Blair didn't say anything, so he continued. "Shane's my best friend, and he's a great guy, but he really doesn't know what he wants yet. At least not when it comes to girls."

"So?"

"Well, Margie does," said Charlie flatly. "I've known her a long time, Blair. She's not really so bad, you know. I don't think she's too sure of herself, and she comes on so strong to hide it."

Blair wanted to tell Charlie to mind his own business, and that Margie was plenty sure of herself. But she knew that Charlie was only trying to be nice, and she really didn't want to talk to him about Shane anyway.

"Well, thanks for the advice, Charlie—and the ride. You're a good dancer."

She got out of the car and went inside.

Chapter Five

The next morning, Blair woke up thinking about how it had felt to dance with Shane. As she showered and dressed, she daydreamed about what it would be like to be his girlfriend.

"I gather you had a nice time last night," her mother said when she came downstairs, humming happily. "You're in such a good mood today. Charlie must be good company."

Blair didn't want to say anything about Shane yet, so she just nodded.

Later in the afternoon, her father asked her about the party, too. "I'll bet those boys were tired last night."

"Well, the party did break up pretty early, but everyone was dancing like crazy until then. You should have seen Charlie."

Her parents smiled at each other. *They prob-*

ably think I have a crush on Charlie, she thought. And that was OK with her. She would tell them about Shane later. Peter, however, was not so easily fooled.

"So, Bean, did you see Shane?" He made kissing sounds at her.

Blair gave an exaggerated sigh. "Maybe you didn't notice, Peter, but I went to the party with Charlie.

"Yeah, and with Frances, too. I heard you telling her on the phone that you didn't want it to look like you were Charlie's date."

"Oh, Peter, mind your own business! And would you *please* stop listening in on my telephone calls!"

Mrs. Young shook her head with an amused smile, but Blair felt like throwing something at Peter.

On Monday, Blair could hardly wait until it was time for rehearsal. She was not only excited about starting to work on the play, but she was also looking forward to seeing Shane again. She wonderd how he would act around her, especially since he would be working so closely with Margie. After school, she rushed over to Mr. Stanley's classroom. She was the first person to arrive.

"Hi, Mr. Stanley," Blair said. "Are we going to work here today or go over to the auditorium?"

"I think we'll do a read-through here today," he replied. "Then we'll meet in the auditorium tomorrow."

Blair looked out the window. She didn't want to sit down until Shane came so she could find a seat next to him. Fortunately, he, too, was one of the first to get there.

"Hi, Blair. Ready to go?" he asked, walking over to her.

"Yeah, I think so. I know my lines, anyway."

"You know, I'm still not sure about the meaning of some of mine," Shane replied. "Why don't you sit with me. You can help me if I get lost."

"OK," Blair said, sighing with happiness. She and Shane sat at desks across from each other. Before long the other seats filled up. Blair couldn't help cheering quietly when she realized there was no room for Margie anywhere near them.

Charlie and Eric were rather late, but Margie came straggling in last of all.

"Sorry I'm late, Mr. Stanley," she apologized with a phony smile.

"It's OK today, Margie, but since you have a lead role in this play, you, especially, must get to rehearsals on time." His voice was pleasant, but firm. Then he looked around the room and stopped at Blair.

"Blair, would you come up here and sit by me? Since you're going to be the assistant director, I'll need you to help explain some of the lines. Margie, you go sit next to Shane since you have so much dialogue together."

Blair could barely control her disappointment. She stood up reluctantly and walked slowly to the front of the room. She glanced at Margie, who was walking toward Shane with a smug expression on her face.

"OK, everyone," Mr. Stanley called, "let's start from the beginning. Blair, could you get the chorus together? And I'd like Mercutio, Benvolio, and Tybalt to sit together since they have quite a bit of interaction."

The chorus started off, a little sluggishly at first, but Blair could tell the group would be good with practice. All of them had clear, strong voices. In fact, Blair was quite impressed by the reading, and she could tell by Mr. Stanley's expression that he was pleased, too.

After the chorus's lines, they read through the rest of the play, each person reciting his or her particular lines. When they finished, everyone sat back and began discussing their mistakes and misinterpretations. Mr. Stanley had cut in to explain someone's lines here and there, but all in all, it had gone well.

"How many of you have read the notes and explanations at the end of your books?" asked Mr. Stanley. His eyebrows rose when all the hands went up. "Well, no wonder you've done so well today."

Frances raised her hand. "But this sure is a frustrating story. It seems so much a matter of bad timing and misunderstandings."

"There you have the essential elements of tragedy, Frances," responded Mr. Stanley. "OK, you guys. I think that's enough for today. It's almost five, and the basketball team has to get over to the gym for practice. I'll see you all tomorrow at the auditorium."

The basketball players jumped up and filed out first. Blair watched Charlie and Shane horse around as they left. Then she gathered up her things and looked for Frances. Her eyes met Margie's as she searched the room. Blair smiled. For the sake of the play, she was going to try to get along with her. But Margie looked away. Blair shook her head. It wasn't going to be easy.

"Ready to go, Blair?" Frances asked quietly.

Blair smiled at her. She was glad she had a kind, gentle friend like Frances. The minute they got outside, Frances turned to Blair with a happy expression.

"You'll never guess what happened, Blair—Eric came and sat with me at lunch."

"Oh, Fran, that's terrific," Blair replied. "I just knew he liked you!"

Frances nodded happily, and Blair wished she were as lucky as Fran. Dancing with Shane seemed like a long time ago now.

The next afternoon, the cast met in the auditorium, and Mr. Stanley suggested they do a read-through on the stage first.

"We will be rehearsing scene by scene and then act by act, but I'd like to see how you feel up onstage, how you would move and read lines without direction. I'll let you go through the entire play without any interruption, taking notes on the most obvious problems." He turned to Blair. "You should take notes, too."

The reading didn't go nearly as well as it had the day before. The freedom of the stage made everyone self-conscious, and they tended to huddle in one small area instead of moving freely and dramatically.

"OK." Mr. Stanley looked up and beckoned everyone down off the stage. "Gather around. I've got a lot to say."

When everyone was seated, Mr. Stanley looked

around at their flushed faces. For many of them, it was the first time they had been onstage other than at the auditions.

"To begin with, I have to say that all of you, except Charlie and Blair, were pretty wooden. That's not unusual at first, but it means that you need to practice your lines somewhere where you can move around. You don't have to be leaping all over the place, but you do need to loosen your movements and be comfortable in a large space. Later, the blocking will help you feel more confident, but in the meantime I suggest you practice your lines in the largest place possible. And double up whenever you can. Practice with other cast members even if you take different roles to help each other out until you are more familiar with your lines."

Mr. Stanley took a deep breath. "Now for the specifics. First of all, I'd like to tell you, Charlie, that I think you're a born actor. I hope you stay with it."

Charlie grinned. "Hollywood, here I come!"

The cast laughed, and it broke the tension. They all knew they hadn't done well, and they listened attentively as Mr. Stanley pointed out the weaknesses in each person's reading.

"Tybalt"—he looked at Jack Kennon—"think of yourself as a scrappy alley cat, always quick to bristle and pick a fight. Pretend you've just lost the league game. How would you feel about the Union City High team members?"

"I'd feel like fighting," retorted Jack.

"Perfect!" said Mr. Stanley. "Benvolio, you're *too* happy. Your name means 'good will' and you are trying to make peace between the Capulets and the Montagues. But peacemaking is a big job, too."

Blair could see that Mr. Stanley was going through the male roles first. He appeared to be saving his Romeo criticism until last. Finally, he turned to Shane.

"Romeo, my friend. Remember that you are in love. This is true love in the truest sense. You must show it."

Blair glanced at Margie. Blair figured that she didn't exactly like the thought that Shane was acting—much less having trouble with it.

"You're a romantic youth," Mr. Stanley continued. "Juliet and your love for her are all you can think of. Remember, Shane, the name 'Romeo' means *lover.*"

Shane let out a slightly embarrassed laugh, and Charlie teased him.

"I guess you need some pointers, old buddy."

Shane just smiled, and Blair looked over at Margie again. She still looked annoyed. Now Mr. Stanley looked at Blair.

"Blair, I want to hear your thoughts on the female roles, but first I want to say that you still need to get into your character a little more. Do you know what the word *garrulous* means?"

"Uh, yes. Someone who talks a lot?"

"Yes. The nurse here is a habitual talker—the kind of person who rattles on constantly. And when no one is listening, she mutters. Of course, there are no actual lines for you to mutter, but you must give that impression."

Blair nodded. "I think I understand. I'll work on it."

"Good. Now, let's hear your observations."

Blair took a deep breath and looked at Pam, who was playing Lady Capulet. "Pam, try to remember that Lady Capulet is very young. She, too, was what we would think of as a 'child bride,' and she does what her husband wants. She is not very sympathetic to Juliet, so you must make her more impatient."

Pam listened and nodded, and Blair went on to Laura, Lady Montague. Both girls responded gracefully to Blair's observations, but when she got to Margie, Blair could see the defensiveness on her face. Criticizing her work would be tricky, so she decided to start by complimenting her.

"I think you've done well with this first reading, Margie. Your voice carries and you're using your body a lot." She paused. Margie looked bored. "But I'm not sure you understand all your lines yet."

"What do you mean?" Margie asked quickly. "Give me an example."

"Well," Blair said carefully, "take the line *'wherefore art thou Romeo?'* What do you think it means?"

"Juliet's looking for Romeo in the garden. What else?" Margie answered testily.

"No," Blair said quietly. "She is asking why he had to be a Montague. You can tell by the next lines that she's worried about the feud." Blair stopped, and the room was silent. Margie turned to Mr. Stanley.

"Is that true?" It was obvious from her tone that she was only half-convinced of Blair's explanation.

"Yes," said Mr. Stanley. "It's one of the most misunderstood lines of Shakespeare, even though it's very well known. It's important to read it with understanding because the following lines support its meaning." He went on to explain the speech thoroughly to Margie, who listened reluctantly. When Mr. Stanley was finished, he asked Blair if she had any more comments. She shook her head.

"OK," said Mr. Stanley. "It's time to quit. Same

time, same place tomorrow." Blair started to leave, but he asked her to wait.

"I'll call you later, Fran," Blair said. Then she waited until the rest of the cast had left.

"Blair, your advice was good. You make a good director." He smiled. "I know it was hard to criticize Margie, but that line had to be explained. If you hadn't done it, I would have."

"I just hope I didn't make her too mad."

"You can't think that way if you're directing, Blair. If an actor wants to do a good job, it's his or her job to listen to criticism and advice."

Blair nodded. "I like helping direct, Mr. Stanley. I didn't think I would, but it gives me another perspective on acting."

"I'm glad, Blair," he responded. "You know, I'm sorry I couldn't cast you as Juliet. I know you would have played the part well, but the audition didn't go well for you, and it would have been obvious favoritism if I had cast you on the basis of those scenes."

Blair wanted to defend herself, but Mr. Stanley continued. "I know now that it was very hard to play against John. That was my mistake, and I apologize."

Blair felt an enormous surge of relief. He *had* understood, and he did think she would have been a good Juliet. Knowing this wasn't as good as being cast, but it was comforting to hear that he had faith in her.

"It's OK," Mr. Stanley. I think you cast the play just right."

"Thanks, Blair. I appreciate your support."

On Wednesday they rehearsed the first scene, which Mr. Stanley blocked for them with Blair's help. By the time the two hours had passed, Benvolio and Romeo knew their lines perfectly and they were both much more relaxed. Mr. Stanley then asked Blair to go up and help Shane on his blocking. She was delighted. They stood close together onstage while she gave him some pointers. He listened to her so attentively that she wanted to reach out and touch him as she left the stage—just as she had seen Margie do at the game. Instead she whispered, "Good luck, Shane."

He smiled. "Thanks, Blair."

When Blair walked off the stage toward her seat by Mr. Stanley, she had to pass by Margie, who stretched her leg out in the narrow aisle. If Blair hadn't been looking down, she would have tripped. Margie looked up and gave her a withering glance.

When rehearsals were over, Margie walked up onstage and took Shane by the arm.

"Come on, Shane. I'll walk to the gym with you."

Blair frowned as she watched them leave.

"I told you he doesn't know what he wants." Charlie had walked up quietly behind Blair. She wheeled around.

"Oh, leave me alone, Charlie!" Blair regretted her sharp words immediately. "I'm sorry, Charlie. I was mad at Margie for trying to trip me. I didn't mean to take it out on you." It wasn't the whole truth, but almost.

"It's OK. This thing with Margie and Shane isn't really my business, but I hate to see you getting involved."

"I'm not involved in anything, Charlie," she answered defensively. "It's just hard working with Margie because she thinks she owns Shane."

"Well, she's not exactly blind, Blair. She wants to go out with Shane, and she sees you as competition. It's as simple as that."

Blair didn't know what to say. "Well, that doesn't mean she has to trip me," she finally grumbled.

"Yeah, it was kinda sneaky. She should have belted you one."

"Oh, Charlie!" Blair laughed.

Rehearsals went fairly well on Thursday, but on Friday, everything fell apart. Margie missed her cues and snapped at Blair during their scene together. Again, Mr. Stanley had to talk to her. He was totally bewildered by Margie's behavior.

"Margie, I don't know where your attitude is coming from. Is it Blair or the role or the nurse that you are reacting to?" The auditorium was completely silent. Even if Mr. Stanley was confused, most of the cast knew what was going on between the two girls. This time, however, Margie was cooperative. She brushed back her dark hair with a light gesture and spoke sweetly. "I'm sorry, Mr. Stanley. I guess I'm not used to having a nurse hover over me."

"Well, don't think of yourself as Margie Mason. For the next few weeks, you must *be* Juliet. Get into her head."

His voice was kinder, but he was growing impatient with her, and Margie knew it.

"Yes, Mr. Stanley," she said softly.

Blair decided it was time she had a talk with Margie. The prospect didn't exactly please her, but Margie's attitude was ruining the rehearsals.

They worked until six that day, and everyone left quickly when Mr. Stanley dismissed them. Blair saw Margie walking up the aisle of the auditorium with Shane. She squared her shoulders and followed them.

"Margie," she called. Margie ignored her and

put her arm through Shane's, drawing him closer.

"Margie!" Blair spoke louder.

Shane stopped and turned around. He looked at Margie. "Blair's calling you."

Margie sighed heavily. "Yes?" she asked as Blair walked up to them.

"Margie, look," Blair began. "We've got to call a truce. You're making the rehearsals difficult on everyone with your attitude toward me." There was a long pause while Margie stared coldly at Blair without responding. Shane looked from one girl to the other.

"She's right, Margie," he said simply.

Margie ignored him and continued to stare at Blair. Finally she spoke. "Look, Blair. You may be the coach's precious daughter, and you may be Mr. Stanley's precious assistant director, but you have no right to criticize me just because you didn't get the part you wanted."

Blair was dumbfounded. How dare she say that! Blair couldn't believe Margie's nerve. Suddenly tears sprang to Blair's eyes. She brushed past Shane and Margie and ran outside. The cold air stung the moisture in the corners of her eyes. She stuffed her hands in the pockets of her jacket and headed for home. *It's no use.* She sighed. *Margie isn't going to let up as long as she thinks I'm interested in Shane.* She was halfway across the campus when Shane came running up to her.

"Blair, wait! I have to talk to you." He fell in step with her.

Blair glanced at him but said nothing. They walked in silence until they got to the edge of the school property.

"Where's Margie?" she asked finally.

"I don't know. On her way home, I guess. I told her that she was acting terribly, and she walked off in a huff."

Blair blinked. For a second she thought she was going to burst into tears, but she got hold of herself and turned to Shane with a smile.

"Thanks, Shane. I appreciate your standing up for me."

"Well, you're right. Margie's been impossible."

"Oh, let's not talk about it. Everything will work out."

Shane continued to walk beside her all the way home. They talked about a lot of things. She told him about the town she had come from and how she had hated moving at first.

"But you like it now, don't you?"

"Yeah, I guess I do—especially because of Mr. Stanley's class." She wanted to say it was because of him, too, but she couldn't. She went on talking about her love of acting instead.

Shane listened closely. Then he told her about his summer job as a camp counselor.

"This year, I'm going to start a basketball team at the camp with Charlie. We've picked up a lot of pointers on coaching from your dad. He really turned our team around with his coaching style."

Blair had relaxed by the time they reached her house. It was easier to talk to Shane than she'd thought it would be.

Blair invited Shane in for a snack, and he accepted. When they walked into the kitchen, Mrs. Young was making dinner. Blair could tell she was surprised to see Shane, but she was as warm and friendly as ever.

"It's nice to see you, Shane. I'm looking forward to tomorrow's game." She wiped her hands on a dish towel. "We're all very optimistic about it."

"So am I," said Shane.

Shane and Blair went into the living room to talk for a while. She had gotten them cookies and milk, and they turned on the stereo. Blair was relieved that Peter wasn't home. She didn't dare ask her mother where he was for fear she would say he'd be back any minute.

Shane sat very close to Blair on the couch, so close that Blair found her hopes soaring. Maybe this was only the beginning! At one point Shane even rested his arm on the back of the couch behind her, and Blair leaned back slightly.

"You've really been a good sport about the play, Blair," Shane said seriously. "I know Margie hasn't exactly made it easy for you, but you're a really good director."

Blair felt her cheeks flush slightly and was almost relieved when her mother came in to ask Shane if he would like to stay for dinner. "Do you like meat loaf and roasted potatoes?" she said.

"Sounds great!" said Shane. "Just let me check with my mom."

Blair showed him where the phone was and then walked back into the kitchen where her mother was preparing the salad.

"Thanks, Mom."

Mrs. Young smiled at Blair. "Your friends are always welcome, honey. And your dad will be glad to see Shane."

Just then, Shane came into the kitchen. "My mom said it's fine for me to stay. Thanks for inviting me, Mrs. Young. I hope I'm not putting you to any trouble."

"Not at all," Blair's mother replied. "I always end up making too much. Actually, you'll be helping me out."

Blair set the table, and Shane helped her. Then, when Peter and Mr. Young both got home, they sat down to eat. Dinner was fun, although basketball seemed to dominate the conversation. But Blair didn't mind listening. She was happy just to have Shane there. It was after nine when Shane finally said he had better get home.

Blair walked out on the front porch with him. He stood on the lower step so their eyes met. The porch light caught the golden glints in Shane's hazel eyes, and Blair was mesmerized. Just then she thought that Shane Lawson was the most handsome boy she had ever seen. Even though the night was cold, Blair felt warm all over.

"Thanks for everything, Blair. I really had fun."

"So did I, Shane."

"Uh, Blair, I was wondering—would you like to go over to the gym after the game? There's going to be a party there whether we win or not."

Blair was so surprised that she couldn't answer right away.

"Oh, were you going with Charlie?" Shane asked.

"No—no. I'm not going with Charlie. I'd love to go with you, Shane."

"Great! I'll pick you up at about seven, OK?"

"OK!"

" 'Bye, Blair." Shane turned and ran down